We are the Champions

Sean McCann

We are
the Champions

Illustrated by Barry Raynor

HODDER AND STOUGHTON
LONDON   SYDNEY   AUCKLAND   TORONTO

British Library Cataloguing in Publication Data
McCann, Sean
 We are the champions.
 I. Title
 823'.9'1J   PZ7.M/

ISBN 0-340-19115-5

Contents

CHAPTER I

'*Who ever heard of Drove's End?*'

'Did you see the paper?' Roy Carew asked as he burst into the hut of Drove's End Boys Football Club.

The three other lads sitting around in various stages of putting on their gear looked up quickly. The blank looks on their faces was enough to show that they really hadn't a clue what Roy was on about.

Roy thrust the paper forward. 'We're playing Brimsley Boys in the final of the County Cup.'

'The what cup?' asked Jimmy Evans.

'Brimsley Boys!' Hugh Richards' voice was more like a bell tolling doomsday. 'Brimsley Boys.'

'They won the League in the south of the county and as we were the winners up here we play them for the County Cup.'

The headline, small even by local standards said 'Brimsley Boys to play Drove's End.' Roy read the item:

'"Brimsley Boys, unbeaten local schoolboy team for the past year look like adding another trophy to their already fine collection when they play Drove's End Boys in the County Cup final.

'"Drove's End, surprise winners of the Fenland Under-15 League this season, are not a great force and will find the formidable combination of the local Town boys, guided by councillor, butcher and grocer, Mr Ed Bradshaw, much too strong for them. Mr Bradshaw is not at all worried by the opposition even though he asked our reporter 'Where is Drove's End?'"'

'The blooming cheek of them', interjected Tony Merton.

'That's not all,' said Roy. 'Listen to this.' He started reading again. ' "Mr Bradshaw has already lined up the necessary travel permits for his team for France . . . This trip is an added incentive to the County Cup winners who play in Europe for the Twin Town Trophy. Mr Bradshaw said today: 'We will do well in Europe!' " '

The four of them just looked at each other. Then Pat Lucas laughed, loud and hearty.

'Wouldn't it be a great joke if we were the champions', he said in between laughs.

'And who says we won't?' answered Jimmy Evans.

'Just give me half a chance to show the Brimsley mouth shooters what I think of them.'

'Don't worry you'll get your chance.' This time the voice came from the door and they looked up to see Sam Nelson, their trainer, coach, manager and general factotum come in.

'You've seen the paper then?' said Roy.

Sam nodded.

'And what do you think?' asked Jimmy.

'It isn't what I think,' Sam replied. 'Let's say it's more what you do.'

The four looked at each other.

'Brimsley Boys are what you might call a living legend in their own area. Since they were ten they have been playing together – and they have won just about every league and championship you can name. Someone said that Bradshaw expects them to be playing in senior football before they are seventeen – then he hopes they will all make Brimsley Rovers in the Third Division.'

Sam stopped and looked around the boys sitting on the bench.

'But', he said, with a sudden grin, 'into every life a little rain must fall.'

At that moment back in Brimsley, councillor, butcher and eminent grocer Edward Bradshaw was sitting in a restaurant with three colleagues from the council.

'You saw the paper then?' he asked, the loud voice meant for more than his immediate company. 'You saw where the lads are getting ready for the Twin-Town cup.'

'Ay', said one of the other men, 'but haven't you to play another match?'

'True', said Bradshaw. 'But that's no problem. Drove's

End!' His round red face, split in laughter. 'Have you ever heard of Drove's End? And what would they say over in Bruges if they had to play Drove's End. Drove's End', he started eating, but could hardly control the laugh. 'Oui, monsiuer Drove's End from ze Fens.'

His French accent wasn't the best but it was enough to make his companions smile.

'I've been a councillor in this county for thirty years and I don't even know where Drove's End is.' He ate another mouthful. 'Do any of you?'

Two shook their heads but the third man looked up. 'It's over beyond Sutton. Back of beyond. I'm surprised they have enough lads to make a team. But I'll tell you this, last year they won their League.'

'League', spluttered Bradshaw. 'That end of the Fens would produce a mountain before it would produce a footballer.'

'I'd not be too sure', came the reply. 'There was a lot of talk about a lad called Goode, Georgie Goode, last year. A diddycoy whose father stopped in a field by the common. They said he would win anything . . . on his own.'

Bradshaw laughed. 'Did they then? Goode you say. Wait till my lads get him. Goode for nothing it'll be.' He laughed and went back to eating. 'Brimsley for Europe', he said, 'you wait and see!'

The confidence was still showing itself plainly on his face as Edward Bradshaw pushed open the door of the restaurant and almost collided with a tall, black haired, red faced man about to enter.

'Ah, Mr Bradshaw', said the man, 'well fed then? You look as though you had just had a slice off the golden egg that the goose laid.'

Bradshaw looked up and laughed.

'You might say that, Moffatt', he said. 'Saw your piece in the paper about the next match my boys have to play.'

'The County Cup?'

'That's right', answered Bradshaw. 'Shouldn't be too much trouble for us would you say?'

'Not on the face of it', replied Moffatt, 'but there are suggestions from the north end of the county that Drove's End are quite a compelling team when they get into their game.'

'You could say the same about my boys', Bradshaw boomed and smiled widely at a couple of people who passed into the restaurant. 'It takes a lot to beat Brimsley Boys . . . as we've shown over the years.'

'Yes indeed', agreed Moffatt, 'I haven't seen the

Drove's End team but our correspondent over there tells me they are much better than people generally realise.'

'If they're all that good why haven't we seen more about them in your paper?' Some of the geniality was leaving Bradshaw's face. He was hearing too much now about Drove's End. 'After all you are sports reporter on the *Chronicle* . . . isn't it your job to keep the public informed?'

'Well we don't by-pass the news when it's there – but schoolboy football doesn't have the greatest following in this part of the world.'

'Say that again', Bradshaw glowered, 'if my boys were to win the F.A. Cup you'd hardly recognise it at the *Chronicle*.'

'That's not really fair', interjected Moffatt, 'there's hardly been a week when you haven't had a mention and if I remember correctly the team's picture has been in there often enough.'

'Well we'll give you the chance of putting it in again – after the cup', said Bradshaw, 'you will have to acknowledge our county championship win.'

'I'm sure we will', Moffatt smiled wryly and moved to go into the restaurant. But he couldn't let the opportunity slip of having a dig at Bradshaw. 'But will you want it in if you lose?'

Bradshaw bridled and took a half step after the reporter. 'Look after yourself, Moffatt, local pride means a lot in Brimsley, and there are some people with a fair share of local pull who carry a lot of weight. I wouldn't upset them if I were you.'

'I suppose the important thing, Mr Bradshaw, is that you are not me', Moffatt opened the door and then half turned again. 'I might just go over to Drove's End on

Saturday and see what sort of a team they have. Wouldn't that create some local interest?'

'If you give them publicity you will give the same to us!' Bradshaw's face was turning an all over lobster shade of red. 'If you don't you'll be sorry.'

But Moffatt had gone in and the door shut gently on its spring hinge, leaving Bradshaw looking at his own reflection in the glass.

All the way back across the square and down a couple of short narrow streets Councillor Bradshaw thought about what had just happened. He wasn't used to being laughed at – yet that was just what Moffatt had been doing, to his face. It upset him and he knew he was upset. But he felt he was upset with justification. Local papers should give local support yet here was Moffatt suggesting that he might write something about the opposition. These young reporters just didn't realise his pull, his important place in Brimsley. Didn't Moffatt know the *Chronicle* could not afford to annoy a leading advertiser and a leader in local affairs?

As well as that Moffatt should realise that Brimsley Boys were poised for their greatest ever game . . . a game that could open new horizons for his boys. The irritation began to disappear as he thought of his team.

There just couldn't be a team anywhere with the cheek to believe they could beat Brimsley Boys.

He began to weigh up all the things in favour of Brimsley.

They had been together for four years . . . and although he had brought in a few players during those years they were basically the same team that had started out under his guidance the year he was Mayor.

They were strong in every position . . . strong enough

to have gone a whole season without a single defeat.

Football in the Fens was an art that had never got beyond a place in the Southern League while the 'more sophisticated residents of his town' (these were Councillor Bradshaw's own words) knew what good soccer was all about. After all Brimsley had a team in the third division.

And the final point that he made to himself during his lunch time walk was, in his opinion, the important one— Brimsley Boys would be playing the match in their own town on the Rovers' ground. And then finally as he walked into his shop he muttered, 'Who ever heard of Drove's End'.

The thought was enough to lift some of the irritation caused by the meeting with Moffatt.

'No team', he told himself once again, 'would have the cheek to beat Brimsley Boys.' He had convinced his team of this – and, more important, he believed it himself.

During the afternoon as he dealt with the problems of his butcher's shop and the grocery business there was a thought that kept coming back into focus – who ever heard of Drove's End? It was such a persistent question that he went to the phone and made a call.

'Brimsley Rovers F.C.' said a voice at the other end.

'Put me through to the manager of the reserves, Joe Sherman', ordered Councillor Bradshaw.

A moment's delay. 'That you Joe, this is Mr Bradshaw here. Joe, ever heard of a team at Drove's End?'

There was an immediate response from the phone, preceded by a sniff and a cough. 'Heard of them! I'll say I have! A team I've got nothing good to say about – or about Sam Nelson who runs them. I've had a few meetings on the football field with Nelson when we played in the Lancashire League.'

Bradshaw's frown turned to a half smile as he heard Joe's comment about Nelson. 'Look Joe I would like you to do something for me . . .'

'Now, Mr Bradshaw, I've helped you out before and you said after the last job you wouldn't want me any more.'

'But I do, Joe,' Bradshaw spoke intently and slowly into the phone. 'I want you to do this job for me.' He brushed aside the words starting to come through. 'You'll do it for me Joe. Come round and see me tonight.'

CHAPTER 2

'*I'll make you an offer*'

'I don't want anyone to forget that this is a friendly game. I want you to play for the enjoyment of it. I don't want anyone to take unnecessary risks. The big game is only a couple of weeks away. This one is to keep you in trim and nothing else.'

Sam Nelson stood in the hut and looked at the Drove's End team sitting on the benches. The all white strip was a tribute to Sam's wife who obviously knew the right washing powder to use.

'No heroics', warned Sam. Then he looked directly at Christy May. 'And no messing about. Let's all play football all the time.'

It was a good day for playing football; enough sun, enough warmth and enough give in the ground. Sam stood on the halfway line and shouted whatever instructions he felt he had to give. On the other sideline was the man who managed Nene Rovers, Roy Cole. He was an old friend of Sam's and had suggested this game between his team from Peterborough and the lads from Drove's End.

Apart from the two men there were about half a dozen boys standing round watching. The game was nothing to get excited about. Drove's End were playing a lively game. The ball travelled quickly from player to player, being picked up by the boy it was intended for and carried into the Nene Rovers' area. But it didn't get far past the visitors' defence until the game was nearly fifteen minutes old. Then a quick raid, different from their early tactics put Drove's End away. The ball was put inside the Rovers' full back and there was Georgie Goode, hair flying in all directions, running on it and chipping it gently over the advancing keeper's head right into the top far corner of the net.

Sam applauded and just then realised that on the far side of the field there was a new figure. The slight stooping figure wrapped up in a long overcoat was standing alone and applauding quietly.

The stranger looked across at Sam and then hunched himself deeper into the big coat. Sam felt that there was something familiar about the man. But he couldn't place it. He cast occasional glances across the field in between shouting at the team. But Drove's End were winning easily; coasting away from the visitors. Three goals up at half time and not much to worry about.

Two more came from the educated feet of Georgie before the game was much older.

Sam never ceased to be amazed at this youngster. Still in his first season of playing football it was his skills that had won the League's under-15 competition for Drove's End. When Georgie first came to the village he had been something of an enigma. You couldn't really be sure what was going to happen next but as the games went on and the season progressed Sam could see a more settled player emerging.

It was the final League game that made Georgie – no doubt about that. Drove's End won it well to clinch the League and it was Georgie's game. Yet Sam wasn't slow to give credit to the rest of the lads who played with so much enthusiasm. They could easily have turned against Georgie – for a number of reasons.

Georgie was a newcomer to the area and lived in a caravan at the bottom of the football field with his father who was a dealer in old furniture and the like. He was quiet, withdrawn at times and yet could be as arrogant as anyone when he felt like it. He was a great concoction of enthusiasm, arrogance, placidness and, on the football field, grace and speed. Sam could tell when Georgie was about to streak into action – he smouldered for a few minutes and showed signs of restlessness. Then he would spring to life and it took a good defence to stop him.

As far as Sam was concerned Georgie had the makings of a great player – but always at the back of his mind was the feeling that just as Georgie could be great so too could he be very wayward.

It was something, Sam felt, that would show itself to the young player's disadvantage one day.

For all that the advent of Georgie was the best thing that had ever happened to Drove's End. From a team of nonentities they had blossomed into one of the best combinations in the area . . . and they would stay that way while they had Georgie.

Thinking of this Sam forgot the stranger on the opposite sideline – until well into the second half of the game.

Then he noticed the man again . . . because whenever Sam moved to a place that put them opposite each other the man moved away, even though it meant moving at times to a place well behind the goal area.

When the final whistle went Drove's End were good and easy winners by five clear goals. Three to Georgie, and one each to Derek Quick and Brian Munroe.

'Well played, lads', said Sam as he went into the hut for a minute before leaving to talk to the Nene Rovers team and their manager.

'You've a good team there', said Roy, tall, bushy haired and once a good player in local football. 'And that Georgie — I'm not surprised he caused so many upsets in the League last season. He looks well out of his class here.'

'He had a good game', said Sam. 'But wait till he gets used to playing in the boots and then see how much he'll improve.'

'What do you mean?'

'Well up to now he hasn't been able to wear boots and settled for plimsolls. But since the League win we have kept him to the boots and it has made a difference to him. He still hasn't really settled into them.'

With that the door of the Drove's End team opened and Georgie hurried out.

'You're off quick, Georgie,' said Sam, as the tall lithe lad came out. 'What's the rush?'

'Got to help', said Georgie. 'There's work for me at home.'

And without waiting to get further acknowledgement from the manager Georgie ran off. Sam watched him go — and Roy Cole laughed.

'A lad who makes his own way in life', he said.

'You can say that again', said Sam, watching the

running figure. Then Sam noticed something else. Far down the field, near to where the Goode's caravan was parked the man in the long coat was blocking Georgie's path.

From the distance Sam saw the man stop and wait in the path of the running boy.

'I wonder what's on there?' he said to Roy.

'Where?' asked the Nene Rovers manager. And Sam pointed down the field.

'That man down there, he was at the game and stayed for the whole match. He seems to have something to say to Georgie.'

'Probably a Manchester United scout', laughed Cole. 'They could do with a player like Georgie!'

Sam said nothing. He was racking his brain to try and place the man . . . because he knew well that this was no real stranger. More and more he felt he had seen him somewhere before.

'You don't know him, do you?' he asked.

'Well I didn't pay much notice to him during the game', said Roy, 'I was too busy trying to stop your lads scoring.'

He squinted against the sun looking now at the two figures stopped in conversation at the far end of the field.

'No, I don't think I know him,' said Cole. 'But if you transfer your lad to some big club let me know and I'll sell you a few of ours.'

Georgie wasn't a lad who was surprised by anyone's approach . . . he had been around the country and had come face to face with most situations. He had noticed the man at the match but had paid no attention to him. Now as the man moved across towards him he stopped running.

'Good game lad', said the man, a small hard, closely cropped head peering out of the top of the big dark overcoat. He took out a packet of cigarettes. 'Have a smoke.'

Georgie shook his head.

'Lucky lad', muttered the man taking a cigarette as if by second nature and putting it in his mouth. 'Don't ever start . . . and you won't finish up like me. I can't give them up!'

Georgie could well understand this. The fingers were dark brown with nicotine.

'You played well', said the man, 'but you're out of your class there. How would you like to play for a real team?'

He looked quizically at Georgie who stood a good ten inches taller than him.

'It would be worth your while', went on the man, quite unaware that so far Georgie hadn't said a word. 'There's incentives these days you know.'

He pulled hard on the cigarette letting the smoke drift away into Georgie's face. Georgie coughed and the man turned away.

'Don't like the old fags at all then', he said, 'you're the sort of lad we want. There's a team not far from here who would like you to play for them. And there's the money incentive.'

He noticed this time there was a reaction from Georgie. A sudden lift of the head and a frown from the lad.

'Money', he said. 'And you'd be taken to and from every match and there's a lot of little things on the side.'

'What team is this?' asked Georgie.

'Well that's something you'd find out later. Agree to sign for them and then I'll tell you everything.'

'You must be cuckoo!' Georgie's explosion of words surprised the man. 'Sign for someone I don't know, for something I am told about like this.'

'The something is what's more important isn't it', the little man eyed Georgie and lit up another cigarette from the one now only half smoked through. 'A handy fifty pence a week for you starting now.' He took a fifty pence piece from the depths of the coat pocket. 'Handy money for a lad of fifteen.'

'Is this some sort of leg-pull?' Georgie was becoming more and more surprised at the conversation.

'No leg pull, lad. There's a team that you would fit in

with very well and I've been asked by them to make this offer to you. What do you say?'

Georgie said nothing but started to move away towards the caravan. The man stood still.

'You won't be making a mistake if you sign', he said, 'there's a big future for young footballers these days. What do you say?'

'All this for fifty pence', Georgie stopped and turned and looked at the man, 'if that's talking money you can't be asking me to sign for Derby or Stoke.'

'Look, son, don't get me annoyed, I've come here to make you an offer and you won't sneer at me', the man crouched again in the coat. 'Smart alecks get nowhere. What do you say to my offer . . .'

'Just that I think you're talking to the wrong person, mister', Georgie walked on again.

'You might be sorry you didn't listen', it was a thin quiet voice that surprised Georgie but he kept on walking and didn't look back.

He didn't see the little man cross the field, then cast an ugly look at the departing footballer.

Nor did he see Sam Nelson at the far end of the field still looking down at the two of them wondering what was going on . . . but never suspecting that there was another team interested in signing Georgie. If he had known he wouldn't have stood there so quietly.

CHAPTER 3

'A cocky little devil'

'Well', said Bradshaw, not bothering to look up from the ledger in front of him on the desk. 'Well, Joe, you fixed it.'

Joe Sherman stood fidgeting in front of the big man, not sure where to start.

Bradshaw looked up, narrowing his eyes in his otherwise big moon-open face. 'Well, Joe', he spoke quietly. 'You did as I said.'

'Oh, I did that all right, Mr Bradshaw', Joe said quickly. 'But it wasn't as easy as we thought.'

'What do you mean it wasn't as easy as we thought?'

'A cocky little devil this Georgie Goode', said Joe. 'Sneered at me . . . and nearly laughed when I offered him the fifty pence a week just to sign.'

Bradshaw didn't look happy with Joe's statement.

'I tried Mr Bradshaw', Joe hurried through the words. 'Honest I did, but he's a cocky little devil. It'll be hard to get him away from Drove's End. The father's a diddycoy . . . got a caravan beside the football pitch and then there's big Sam Nelson . . .'

'You're not still afraid of big Sam', Bradshaw laughed. 'It was years ago when you two last met.'

'I know, Mr Bradshaw, but Sam might soon get to know who was after his lad. Not that it makes any difference . . . I wouldn't mention your name to him . . . or to anyone else.'

'I'm sure you wouldn't, Joe.'

'He's a good player all the same,' there was just a touch

of admiration in Joe's voice. 'He could make the final awkward for Brimsley Boys.'

'No gypsy is going to make things tough for my boys', Bradshaw's voice rose shrilly as he got up and banged a fist on the desk. 'No gypsy . . . no other team is going to stop Brimsley Boys.'

He paced across and looked out the window. Joe started to light up a cigarette. When he heard the match striking Bradshaw looked around.

'Put that thing out . . . those cigarettes you smoke are foul . . . they smell like paper and dung.'

With a stuttered apology Joe pushed the cigarette into a black ash-tray on the desk.

Bradshaw turned back towards the window and looked out. 'Laughed at fifty pence did he then', muttered the big man. 'Ought to have realised how well off he would be. Did you say anything about anything else?'

'No, Mr Bradshaw', Joe replied.

'You didn't offer him the track suit or the gear bag?'

'He was such a cocky devil . . . and there was something odd in the way he looked at me', Joe gave a little shiver at the memory. 'He has funny eyes and a head of long hair . . . and the way he laughed at the money. Implied we must be the last of the big spenders . . . he wanted to know if we were competing in the big money stakes with Stoke and Derby.'

'That sort is he', said Bradshaw. 'We've got better players away from other clubs for a lot less.'

Bradshaw turned back from the window and sat at the desk. 'Well, Joe, what would you say you do now?' He looked at the long coated little man in front of him. 'Could you be more persuasive?'

'Ah, now Mr Bradshaw', Joe felt the cold shiver run from the back of his knees to the nape of his neck. 'You know my strength. Gentle persuasion . . . I'd be no good at anything else.'

'Now, Joe, we've had little arrangements before. I'm sure another wouldn't be beyond your scope.'

Bradshaw was enjoying watching the little man visibly squirm in front of him.

'You've got one or two "heavy" lads in Brimsley Rover's reserve team haven't you?'

Joe nodded.

'Well I might want some of those to play in a team for

me', Bradshaw laughed again as the plan began to formulate in his mind. 'There's a sort of sponsored tournament play-off that will interest Drove's End . . .'

Sam saw the first notice of the match in the paper – before he got the letter. It announced that Drove's End would meet a team called the All Blues in the play-off for the Cordial Sponsored Tournament at Drove's End ground the following Saturday.

The letter when he read it that evening said much the same thing. The Cordial Sponsored Tournament was for a plaque to be awarded by a prominent businessman who preferred to remain anonymous.

'Who'd have thought when we were winning the League that we would be so sought-after', mused Sam as he went to take that evening's training session. He now had the team training three nights a week in preparation for the county final. He really didn't want another hard game before the big one but, well, he shouldn't turn down the chance of giving the lads another crack at a trophy.

The boys had seen the notice in the paper and were all ears as Sam read out the letter.

'Europe here we come', shouted Benny May as he threw the ball up in the air and caught it almost dead on the instep of his boot.

But goalkeeper John Macken was just a little chary. 'Who are we supposed to play in this game?' he asked.

'Well the letter says they're a team from Norfolk', said Sam.

'I suppose that could be anyone – even the Canaries themselves!' said Benny May.

'Blue canaries', retorted Derek Quick.

There was a general chuckle of laughter – but Sam was

not joining in . . . he was looking at Georgie, head bent
over the boots, still trying to get the hang of tying them
correctly. Georgie hadn't said anything . . . and seemed
far away from the general trend of the enthusiasm of the
rest of the team.

Sam hurried the players up to get them out of the hut.
Georgie wasn't making a great hand of tying the boots.

'You'll need a lesson or two there', said Sam and the
boy's head jerked up. The look he gave Sam was one the
manager had experienced a couple of times before . . . and

whenever he saw this look on Georgie's face it not only gave him the shivers – it worried him.

'I'll teach myself', and as he spoke Georgie's eyes never strayed from a direct gaze at Sam.

For just an instant Sam stood there. 'O.K.', he said 'but let's be having you outside quick.'

As he walked out Sam knew well that Georgie was still looking at him with those piercing eyes.

Sam was out in the field for a few minutes before Georgie emerged. He had changed back into his ordinary clothes and was carrying the boots. Outside the hut he turned and instead of going on to the field, walked away.

'What's the matter with him?' asked Brian Munroe.

No one answered for a minute, as they watched Georgie disappear out of the ground.

'Maybe he's got a touch of the bigheadness', said Benny May. 'Now that someone else wants to sign him he thinks he's above training with us.'

Sam wasn't sure that he had heard correctly. He had been too busy watching Georgie leave the ground. He spun around on Benny.

'What did you say?'

'I just said that he is getting too bigheaded for us now that someone else wants him to sign.'

'Who wants him to sign?'

'Oh, I don't know', said Benny looking down at the ground, knowing well he had said something that was out of turn.

'Well why say something you don't know about', this from Tony Merton.

Benny looked up. 'I do know', he said, looking at Tony.

But he wasn't volunteeing any other information, until Sam pressed him.

'Well, Georgie was telling me that there was a man at the match on Saturday who asked him to sign for another team. That's all.'

'What other team?' Sam remembered again the man and the confrontation after the game.

'He didn't say', said Benny. 'Just that the man asked him to sign on – and it would be worth his while!'

There was a whistle from the back of the group. 'Phew', said Derek Quick, 'I wish someone would make me an offer . . .'

'And we might encourage you to take it', taunted Roy Carew.

But this was more than mere banter to Sam. This had a serious ring about it. He knew that without Georgie the team would have little chance against big-time opposition. It was his own fault – he had relied too much on one player.

He should have realised that word would soon get out about Georgie Goode. There were too many clubs on the lookout for young players, today if they kicked a football they were targets for scouts. An ounce of talent brought offers from all quarters. But somehow he had never thought of it this way before . . . after all Drove's End seemed too far off the beaten track for scouts to pay it any attention.

Who could tell though what motivation was behind the scheme; if it was meant to upset Georgie it had achieved its object.

Sam left the players still bantering about transfers and big offers and walked back to the hut. The old spectre of Georgie seemed to have the label 'trouble' attached to it again. And Sam wasn't sure how to handle it.

Sam's experience with the Goode family had taught him that he had to act very cooly if he wanted to make any headway with them. Georgie was tempermental – but far less so than his father who had been known to explode for the most insignificant reason or comment. He put off going near the family for a couple of nights. But when there was no sign of Georgie at the next training session he decided to take his chance and walked over to the caravan.

The large half bred dog rushed headlong at him but Sam knew that the dog was well tied although he was given a good long lead to keep busybodies away.

'Down dog', he said in a voice he knew lacked the authority of Mr Goode. His knock on the caravan was answered by the big man. It was the first time they had met since Drove's End had been successful in the League.

This time the big man was far more amiable.

'Mr Nelson', he said, 'how's it going?'

'Fine, Mr Goode', Sam knew his words were coming with a certain hesitancy. The dog was still snarling in the background but a quick word from Georgie's father sent him slinking to the end of the line.

'I was wondering where Georgie is?'

'Well, Mr Nelson, that's something I was going to talk to you about. There's no one in . . . come inside.'

Sam followed Mr Goode into the caravan; inside it was as spotless as on the first occasion he had visited it. He took a seat on the bench indicated by the big man.

'Georgie', Sam started to say.

'He's getting all sorts of ideas in his head about wanting to play for someone else', said Mr Goode. 'There was someone offered him money to change teams.'

'So I heard', replied Sam.

'He didn't tell you then?'

'No, but he did mention it to one of the other lads on the team. I didn't think he would take it seriously.'

'Why shouldn't he take it seriously?' There was more than a hint of aggressiveness in Mr Goode's voice. 'Isn't there a fortune to be made today playing football?'

'There is', Sam wasn't sure how to go on – he had long ago found it meant trouble to say the wrong thing where the Goode family was concerned. 'But very few make it through the sort of approach that was made to Georgie.'

The big man leaned in close.

'Everyone has to start somewhere', he said. 'And fifty pence for kicking a ball is fifty pence more than he is getting at the moment.'

Sam was staggered and jerked his head back in surprise.

'Fifty pence?' he managed to say.

'That's what Georgie was offered', Mr Goode said.

Sam almost laughed. Fifty pence was ludicrous. And he knew the Goode's weren't short of money, you only had to look around the caravan to realise that.

'Who made the offer?' Sam was still somewhere in between laughter and shock.

With that a more realistic look came over Mr Goode's face. 'Well', he said running his hand through his black hair. 'That's the strange thing. Georgie doesn't know. You see he thought someone was pulling his leg . . . but the more he thought about it the more it seemed as though he had turned down a good opportunity.' Mr Goode laughed. 'Mind you he realised that fifty pence was an insult more than an offer but he was upset that he didn't find out who the man was who made the offer.'

Mr Goode laughed again and Sam knew then that the big man was on his side again.

'I realised that Georgie would be upset for not talking out the deal with the man who offered it. After all the Goodes never turned their backs on a potential good deal before this . . . but Georgie is off these past few evenings trying to see if he can find the man who made the offer.'

The relief showed on Sam's face.

'I thought maybe he had signed on for someone else.'

'Don't let that worry you', Mr Goode laughed. 'Georgie is only annoyed that he was so much taken by surprise that he missed out on all his dealing upbringing. I can tell you that when your team wants him he'll be there. I'll see to that.'

CHAPTER 4

'A place for the action'

When Georgie set out to check up on the man and the offer he had no idea where to look. Local buses took him to King's Lynn, Peterborough and on the third night to Brimsley. He reckoned it was worth the try to look around the grounds of the football clubs in his area . . . but by the same token he knew that if he was to keep going he would have to look at Cambridge City, Norwich and even down to Ipswich. And such a search was certainly not on – even though it meant salvaging lost pride with his own family.

'Never look a gift horse in the mouth', was his grandfather's advice . . . and it was advice that his father had commended to him time and time again. But then they had never said that he should bargain his own life away. Now he was searching for the little man . . . and he knew that he might as well be searching for a needle in a haystack.

Brimsley Rovers Football Club was quiet. But there were some lights flickering in the offices under the stand and a wicket gate was open.

He walked up to the gate and through a passageway that led on to the playing field. It was deserted. He stood and looked around. So this was the pitch where Drove's End would be playing on in a couple of weeks time when they lined up against Brimsley Boys.

It would certainly be a change from the grounds they were used to playing on. Brimsley Rovers were a good third division club with a loyal following of a few thousand supporters and their ground was regarded as one of the best in the division.

Georgie was still looking with a certain amount of awe at the ground when he heard a man coming up behind him. He turned just as the man reached him.

'What do you want, son?' the man, well dressed and with trilby pulled down over his forehead looked at him.

Georgie was taken aback for just an instant. But part of the old dealing motto came back to him – 'never be lost for words', his grandfather said.

'I'm looking for a man. I thought I might find him here.'

'What man?'

'Well I don't know his name . . . and he mightn't have anything to do with this club . . . but he wanted me to sign on for his team.'

'And what makes you think it might be Brimsley Rovers?' the man stood his ground blocking any retreat Georgie might make down the tunnel.

'Nothing really', Georgie hesitated. 'He was a little man in a long coat', even as he said it Georgie knew it sounded very lame. Then he remembered something else. 'And he smoked a lot.'

33

The man laughed. 'Ah, it's Smokey Joe you want. That'll be him . . . he runs the reserves here. You'll find him down the end of the corridor', he pointed to another part of the stand. 'He's got a couple of lads with him there.'

Georgie stepped out on the ground and felt a sudden inclination to run on the grass. He took a sprint along the touchline, feinted as if he had the ball at his feet and then kicked as if to send the ball curling towards the top of the net. He could almost see it all happening and felt like letting out a cheer of delight as he visualised the ball dropping over a goalkeeper's clutching fingers into the back of the net.

He turned towards the stand and realised that the man was still in the tunnel watching him. The man lifted his hand in acknowledgement and shouted 'If it was always as easy it would be all right.'

Georgie felt a sudden elation. This was a place to play football . . . this was where the action was . . . a long way from Drove's End. But then he thought of the fifty pence and it changed his tune. 'I wonder what sort of transfer fee they would really pay', he asked himself – not for the first time since the approach had been made.

Through a short tunnel, down a corridor and there was a light in a room with the door slightly ajar. His approach made no noise on the rubber covered floor and just as he reached the door he heard the voices.

'And there's this cocky little beggar', the unmistakeable voice of Joe was saying. 'Clobber him and you're as good as on double bonus money.'

He was so surprised that the rest of the words were lost on him. He stood still and started to move back. But it got too much for him . . . he moved towards the door and through the glass panel saw the figure of Joe, his back

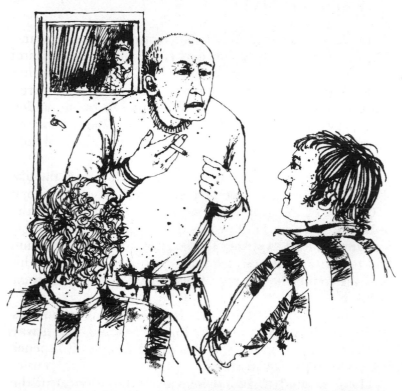

towards him, his head wreathed in cigarette smoke. In front of him sitting on a bench were two players still in the blue and white stripes of Brimsley Rovers. They were looking intently at Joe.

'It doesn't matter how much you're beaten by – after all it's only a scratch team – as long as you do that smart alec, Goode.'

'But what's it worth, Joe?' The heavy face of one of the players looked at him.

'What about a couple of quid each?'

'A couple of quid! You must be joking!'

Georgie gave the lad credit for being a dealer.

'Look, everything's fixed. No trouble, I promise you. A quick job and then you can come off at half time or whenever you manage to clobber him.'

'Look Joe, a fiver each. No less.' Joe turned and Georgie ducked. He turned, took off and ran out of the tunnel faster than he had ever thought possible. Behind him he heard a door slam but didn't look to see whether someone was coming or going in the room.

All he knew was that he had heard a lot more than he should have heard . . . and no bargain was worth an injury.

Georgie didn't stop running until he reached the front of Brimsley Town Hall just in time to jump on to the bus for Drove's End. Another few seconds and he would have had to wait for an hour for the next bus. Somehow he felt that the sooner he got out of Brimsley the better it would be for him.

'A cocky little beggar', the words still rang in his ears. Sitting in the back seat of the bus he realised that he was being set up and so too was the whole Drove's End team. Set up for what? And why?

There seemed to be no logical explanation at all for someone wanting to have a go at him or, to use Joe's own words, 'to clobber' him. One meeting with Smokey Joe could not have in any way been responsible for building up such antagonism.

Smokey Joe had meant nothing to him even on the day they first met after the game with Nene Rovers. If anything he seemed a bit of a laugh, and Georgie remembered that he thought it was something of a joke when he was first approached. Thinking back he knew now that he should have realised that there was something strange, even sinister about the heavy overcoated figure. But the fifty pence . . . that was still a joke surely.

'If only I'd waited and talked to him then', he said to himself as the bus drove across the town and off for the Fens. More than ever now he realised that brushing-off Smokey Joe was a mistake. And if he had only remembered his father's advice 'never turn your back on a deal until you know what it's all about' he would not be in the present situation.

And what could he do now? The options seemed fairly straightforward . . . he could continue to play for Drove's End or forget football altogether or at least until his father decided to move on to some new district.

He didn't want to leave Drove's End, he really was enjoying football and he knew that he had a lot to thank Sam Nelson for. Sam had put him on the right road and was one of the few people who did not nag at him when things went wrong. In football Sam was the sort of man that kept you enjoying your game. He would put things right when they went wrong; he would praise but seldom criticise and while his voice was loud on the field of play he was one of the few people in Drove's End to show the slightest interest in the football team.

They were close to Drove's End when he became aware of a car following the bus. It was the headlights that first caught his attention; then as the bus pulled into each stop the car stayed close behind. There was no sign that the driver wanted to pull out and overtake, though the bus was travelling quite slowly at times and often took minutes at different bus stops.

At one of these stops the car came very close to the back of the bus and Georgie looked closely at it. The light from the bus and the reflected light from the headlights suddenly caught the faces. Sitting beside the driver was the sparrow like figure of Smokey Joe.

The face gave no sign of emotion – just stared straight at Georgie. Suddenly he knew that he had been seen at the ground . . . and that Joe wasn't going to wait for a match for his instructions to be carried out.

He sat it out on the back seat, sitting sideways so that he could see the car behind without it seeming that he was looking at it.

But now the dilemma was really facing him. There was a good walk from the bus stop to the football ground and then across it until he reached the caravan. Plenty of time for Joe and whoever was with him to get in his path and do whatever they wanted to do.

He had never felt fear before . . . well not fear like he felt it now. It was a situation that made his hands feel stone cold and his brow break out in a sweat.

And the reason for such determination on Smokey Joe's part was a mystery to him . . .

His mind turned quickly to some way of escape. He would have to get off the bus – there was no doubt about that . . . out of the bus and away before the men in the car knew what was happening. But always he came back to the realisation that no matter where he decided to get off the bus the car would stop right behind.

There was only one chance of making a fast getaway – he would have to conceal for as long as possible his exit from the bus. He moved from the back seat up towards the driver and sat down in a vacant seat.

'Will you let me out at the common', he asked the driver as they neared Drove's End.

The driver nodded and Georgie looked ahead at the thin ribbon of Fenland road picked out by the bus headlights. He knew when they were coming near the common – it was the only part of the road where there were any hedges. The rest of the road was bounded by dykes and there was hardly a tree in sight. Then the hedges were there, the bus was slowing down.

'Here you are, son', the driver said. But Georgie sat on until the doors had opened fully, then with a leap he left the bus, landed squelching in the soft earth and ran for the gap in the hedge that led on to the common.

The bus was pulling away but he could hear the yell from the car.

'There he goes!' At the same time the door slammed shut and the gabble of raised voices followed him. But he was thankful now that he knew just where the gap was and how best to dodge through the brambles so that they barely touched his faded denim jacket.

But now he could hear the voices muttering curses loudly.

He was through the gap and on to the flat land.

'The brambles . . . I'm stuck', he heard one voice shout.

'Get through and get him', the vicious shout of Smokey Joe couldn't be misunderstood.

But Georgie wasn't interested in what was being said. He had a good head start and he was always fairly fast whenever he had to run. And this was one time he had to run a lot faster than ever before.

Across the ground, through another gap in the common hedge and there was the caravan. He was still a hundred yards away when he let out a shout.

'Get them, dog, get them.'

The sudden shout set the dog wild with barks and baying. The caravan door burst open and Georgie's father stood there in the light.

'What's going on!' The voice raised itself over the wild barking of the dog.

Georgie almost threw himself at the caravan steps. 'Someone behind . . .' he could hardly get the words out. 'After me . . .'

Mr Goode jumped down the steps. Georgie had never seen him move so fast before. He tore at the dog's lead.

'Come on, dog. Get them.' The new found excitement in the life of the big dog sent him crying wild in the night air. Georgie ran behind his father, into the common field. Ahead of them they could just see two figures dashing out through the gap. They ran and the dog pulled wildly at the lead held in his father's hands.

They reached the gap just as the car skidded wildly away from the roadside and sped along the narrow road.

'Shush, dog, shush', Mr Goode bent down and called the dog.

Then he turned to Georgie . . . 'What was that all about?'

Georgie looked at him. 'I don't know', he said and the faltering way he said it made him realise just how lame it must sound to his father.

'You come up to the caravan, shouting at the dog, a wild hunted look on your face, and two men chasing you and you don't know what it's all about!'

His father towered over him. Georgie shook his head and turned to walk back to the caravan. 'It's true', he said, 'I don't know what its all about.'

His father followed him, the dog now quietly ambling beside him.

'Is it something to do with our business or is it something to do with football?'

'It must be the football', said Georgie, 'because one of the men chasing me was the man who offered me the money the other day.'

Mr Goode said nothing more until they were in the caravan. Mrs Goode was there and he told her there had been a little bit of trouble.

'It was hardly trouble', said Georgie.

'Well if that's not trouble my lad I'd hate to see what you call trouble.' Mr Goode sat down on a bench . . . 'Now let's talk about exactly what happened to you.'

CHAPTER 5

'More than meets the eye'

The following evening Georgie and his father met Sam at the ground after training. They told him all that had happened. Sam said nothing until Georgie reached the part where he described the man.

'Always smoking', Georgie said, 'and a man at the ground called him Smokey Joe.'

'Smokey Joe!' Sam cracked his fist into his hand. 'I should have known. Smokey Joe Sherman.'

'You know him?' asked Mr Goode.

'I still have the marks on my legs from the last time we played', Sam rubbed a hand along the calf on one leg, then added with a quiet smile, 'but I think he'll have marks as well.'

'When did it happen?' asked Georgie.

'A long time ago as far as you are concerned', said Sam, 'we played against each other in a game that was the decider in a relegation battle . . . and Joe was out to crock me from the start. The dirtiest little winger that ever wore football boots.'

'Who won?' Georgie asked.

'In the game we won – but in the dirt stakes I would say that the final score between Smokey Joe and myself was just about even.'

'Do you think he is carrying on the personal grudge against you?' Mr Goode asked.

'No, I don't think so', said Sam reflectively. 'No, Joe wouldn't have the mind to think beyond the present moment or to plan a vendetta. There's something more to this than meets the eye.'

He stopped and looked long at the ground while father and son watched him, neither of them speaking.

'I wonder . . .' Sam paused before continuing. 'I wonder if all this has anything to do with the fact that we play Brimsley Boys in the county final.'

'Why would that be so?' asked Mr Goode.

'It's only a wild guess', replied Sam. 'Probably miles from the truth. But it's something we ought to think about. That must have been the match he was talking about. Planning to get some of the Brimsley lads to stop you Georgie and that way get you out of action early in the game.'

'It's a lot of trouble to stop one lad', said Mr Goode.

'But you must remember that they have realised that Georgie knows what's going on. They can't afford to take a chance like that. Georgie is not only the player likely to keep Brimsley out of the chance of going to Europe but he also knows too much.'

'There's a touch of the James Bond about this,' laughed Georgie.

'Well you should know lad . . . after all you were the one who upset their apple cart.' Mr Goode looked at his son, 'and you were the one who didn't think too much about

James Bond when they were chasing you through the fields last night.'

The smile left Georgie's face. The realisation of the situation was getting home to him. He looked at the faces of the two older men. They were tight with worry.

'Well what can I do?' Georgie searched for some help in the faces.

Neither answered for what seemed an age. Then Sam looked down.

'The answer is simple', he said, 'don't play in the game'.

'Don't play', Georgie jumped to his feet. 'Why should I let someone like Smokey Joe or anyone else for that matter stop me playing in the game?'

His father laughed. 'That's what I hoped you'd say! There's plenty of time between now and the county final for us to think about. Isn't that right, Mr Nelson?'

'Right', said Sam, trying to sound cheerful but feeling anything but happy. Only he knew the way Smokey Joe thought and worked . . . and he had the marks to prove it.

'Anyway', he went on, 'there's this other game against the Norfolk team for the plaque tomorrow. Let's start by winning that . . . then we can get down to the Brimsley Boys issue.'

Sam tried to put on the brave face. 'Now what about getting out there and doing the training that you missed out on the rest of the week.'

'Sorry about that, boss', said Georgie and left the hut.

But Sam shouted after him.

'Georgie! I didn't mean that – take it easy, you'll need all the strength you can muster for tomorrow.'

He was left alone then with Mr Goode. The big man had hardly moved his position on the seat from the time the conversation started.

'It's a bit of dirty work, isn't it?' he queried.

Sam nodded. 'Anything that Smokey Joe is involved with is dirty. How he ever got to be trainer of the reserve team at Brimsley beats me. They must be badly off over there.'

'Not all that badly off though', said Mr Goode. 'Georgie said that the Boys team from over there hasn't been beaten for ages.'

'Right', agreed Sam, 'but there's always a first time.'

'You say that with more enthusiasm than conviction', Mr Goode said quietly.

'I have all the best reasons for saying it', Sam answered. 'And there's twelve of them out there practising now.'

He moved towards the door. 'I'll have to give them some of my time. Will you be up for the game tomorrow?'

Mr Goode shook his head. 'I doubt it. I have a load of furniture to move over in Littleport. I mightn't be back in time.'

'Hope you can make it. The support we get for this team is pretty thin on the ground. A shout from the sidelines works wonders.'

With a final acknowledgement of each other the men parted; Mr Goode out of the ground; Sam to the players.

There was a touch of excitement in the air. Benny May came up to Sam, a solemn expression on his dark face. 'That's a bit of bad about Georgie, isn't it?'

Sam looked at him not sure what to say . . . but knowing full well he should have told Georgie to say nothing to the rest of the boys.

'Well we were kidding him about the transfer fee and then he told us that Brimsley were so keen to get him they were trying to kidnap him. Is that right?'

Sam laughed, and hoped it rang true. 'I'd say there was

a touch of your own imagination in the whole thing, Benny', he said. 'Go on, get cracking and let's see what you're made of.'

But it wasn't going to be as easy to dispose of the whole affair. The other players had stopped playing while Benny was talking to Sam. Now they moved over to the two.

Sam realised that something would have to be said. Something that would allay fears – at least until after the plaque game; then they could get down to talking about the Brimsley affair. He was fairly sure that no one would make any sort of approach to Georgie again until next week. Not even Smokey Joe.

But in the middle of his reasoning a thought crossed his

mind . . . so fleeting as to be forgotten quickly but enough to set up a line of worry and fear. And yet the next instant he couldn't think what the thought was.

There was a barrage of questions being thrown at him. He held up a hand at the group of players.

'Look lads', he said, 'someone is playing a naughty game with Georgie. We don't know what it's all about . . . neither does Georgie. But I don't want you to think about it. It will all be sorted out next week. I promise you that. In the meantime there's tomorrow's game.'

'The time is half past eleven sharp here. We kick off at half twelve.'

'Great', came a complaining voice from the back, 'we'll miss the soccer on the telly again.'

'And try and make your parents and friends miss it too', encouraged Sam, 'bring them along. We need support.'

'You can say that again', said Roy Carew.

'Now, lads, let's make it a win tomorrow and put ourselves really on the top rung ready for the big one next week.

'Off with you all now. See you here tomorrow. And you Georgie, no messing about this evening. Straight home.'

'You can say that again, boss', and Sam was pleased to see the smile back on the face of Georgie.

But there was no smile on Sam Nelson's face as he locked up the hut after the boys had gone. There was still the memory of that disturbing thought that flashed across his mind. He couldn't remember what it was . . . but could well remember the effect it had on him.

He tried to think back to the reasoning that had inspired the thought. He had been thinking about the approaches to Georgie and was reasoning that no one would make another approach before tomorrow. That was it . . . no one . . . who else though might be involved beside Smokey Joe? He took up the thread of the reasoning. There must be someone else . . . Smokey Joe hadn't enough initiative to set up anything himself. Somewhere there must be someone who was telling Sherman exactly what to do. Someone who had something more to gain from the game than any of them had realised.

He left the field and walked home trying to think what could anyone gain – other than a mere trophy – from the meeting between the two teams. It wasn't as if there was a fortune involved in the outcome. The only consolation was that he had a week still to find the answer.

CHAPTER 6

'Play it or call it off'

If Sam had to face problems about Georgie and the Brimsley Boys game he was landed with an even greater problem the next morning when he met the team outside the hut before the start of the game. He had been to the ground earlier and with some willing helpers had put up the goalposts and nets and fixed the corner flags. The white strip of Drove's End was as clean as any magic soap powder could get it. Everything looked fixed to Sam.

But he knew that all wasn't well when he saw Derek Quick's face as the captain stood outside the hut.

Without any word of welcome or the time of the day, Derek opened up at Sam.

'Did you see who we've got to play?' he said with a real note of anger in his voice.

'Of course I didn't see who you have to play', Sam snapped back.

'Well wait till you do', said Derek. And with a shake of his head the captain turned back into the hut.

Sam stood for an instant, then decided to find out what was wrong. He walked to the hut reserved for the visiting team, opened the door and looked in. He knew immediately what had worried Derek Quick. Sitting around on the bench wearing an all blue strip were the visitors. Not one of them looked under eighteen.

'Morning', one said, grinding out a cigarette.

Sam nodded. He looked around at the faces that were now turned to him.

'Are you sure you're at the right place?' he asked.

'Hark at him', said one player, 'who do you think you are?'

'I'm in charge of the Drove's End boys', Sam answered stepping into the hut. 'Who's with you?'

'No one at the moment', said another player. 'There'll be a few along later.'

'To feed on the bones of Drove's End', chortled another.

'Shut up, Pete', came the rasping voice from the corner. Sam looked over. A hefty teenager, all of nineteen, looked at him.

'We're here to play your team in the sponsored game', he said. 'All right?'

'Not all right at all', Sam railed at him. 'My lads are only fifteen – you lot must be playing in under nineteen football.'

'No not really', came another voice, 'we were just fed well as babies.'

Sam said nothing. He saw all the makings of a nasty situation staring him in the face.

'What league do you play in?' he asked.

'Oh, a Sunday league – in Hunstanton – a league for teenagers.'

Sam nodded, slowly and backed out of the hut to a gurgle of laughter from behind him in the hut.

The referee came out of the Drove's End hut. Sam asked him about the match – was there an age limit or what did he know about the trophy. The man shook his head; he knew nothing other than the request he had received to referee the game.

'Who made the request?' It was the word request that set Sam thinking.

'It came from Brimsley Rovers football club', replied the referee. 'It was signed by one of their staff.'

Sam immediately suspected the danger. 'Was it Sherman?' he asked. 'Joe Sherman.'

The referee nodded. 'Why', he asked, 'is something worrying you?'

'It is', said Sam emphatically. 'It is . . . it's like throwing a crowd of boys to the lions. Did you see my lads? They're fifteen . . . the team they have to play hasn't a player under eighteen – and that's being generous.'

The referee raised his eyebrows. 'Well', he said, 'that's the chance you take when you decide to play in a tournament like this.'

'I know', said Sam, 'I'm wondering . . .'

But before he could finish the sentence the Drove's End boys emerged from the hut. It was almost a confrontation because at the same minute the All-Blues came out. The older boys stood and looked at their opponents.

One of the visitor's leaned forward and shouted 'Boo'.

'There you are'. said another, 'they don't frighten easily.'

The All-Blues ran on to the field kicking a couple of footballs between them. Drove's End boys stood looking at Sam waiting for him to say something. But for once the big Irishman seemed to be tongue-tied. He looked at them shrugged his shoulder and held out his hands with a look of despair on his face.

'Well', he asked, 'are you going to play them?'

'What's the score, boss?' Georgie had pushed himself forward. 'They are much older than we are. Why?'

'Because', and before he said it Sam knew that he was already on the verge of telling a lie that could change the whole outlook of football for Drove's End, 'because I didn't check up on the tournament. We were entered for it because we won the league . . . there is no age limit. It's a tournament for teenagers.'

He looked at them. 'It's my fault, I should have checked so now it's up to you. Play or call it off?'

Just then the referee whistled shrilly from the centre of the field. The players looked at each other then Pat Lucas threw the ball out in front of them.

'Come on, lads', he said, 'it's only a game.'

There was general agreement and the boys went running on to the field. Only a game – the words kept echoing through Sam's head. He felt completely inadequate and only the referee calling him to run the line brought him out of a near-trance. Just then some men appeared on the field . . . it seemed to Sam as if they came off the bus which had passed the common field just before their appearance.

'Come on the Blues', one voice shouted loudly and three men hurried together to the touchline. A fourth moved off from the main group and walked around the pitch.

There was a swirling wind on the pitch and to make it worse Sam realised that Drove's End would be playing against it in the first half. The teams kicked off but the boys in white took the ball early and quickly. Driving it hard along the ground Jimmy Neil sent it to the feet of Brian Monroe. He took the ball along the touch line while the All-Blues' full back stalked him like a tiger. Just as Brian was about to let the ball loose the full back swooped and without a touch of ceremony landed winger and ball over the line.

Sam was shocked. He shouted 'foul' but was astonished to see the referee give a throw in to All-Blues!

'No way', he shouted. 'It isn't on.'

But from the far touch line there were shouts from the All-Blues supporters. 'Well played ref, you know your job.'

The All-Blues swung the ball solidly now down field. The wind carried it far into the Drove's End half and just on the edge of the box an All-Blues forward, big and hulking, came forward like a heavy tank to take the ball.

But Roy Carew was there first and thumped the ball away.

It was not long out of the danger zone before the big kicking All-Blues sent it back again. Drove's End were sentenced to defence and only Georgie stood up field. Play continued in the bottom half and then there was a shout from the sideline from the stranger walking towards Sam.

'Look out! Centre forward look-out.'

Sam swivelled to look where the man was pointing . . . He was just in time to see Georgie fall to the ground in a swirl of legs. On top of him was the All-Blues centre half, lashing out with boots and fists.

Sam was into his stride with one bound and across the field. He heard the voices from the other side shouting; 'Get him off, ref.' He heard the whistle of the ref. He heard the pounding feet beside him and it was almost second nature to swivel sideways as an All-Blues player

came racing at him. Old training in avoiding full blooded tackles stood well in his stead now. He side stepped but continued to run at the group on the ground.

'Get off him!' he roared as he ploughed into the player in the blue shirt and pulled shirt and hair out of the personal scrimmage.

Another player came towards him and he felt the blow on the back of the neck . . . but he swung and with a sure sense of direction hit the attacking player high in the chest.

Suddenly all hell seemed to break loose. Players ran pell mell at the group; the referee whistled continuously and Sam threw himself over Georgie just in time to stop another boot finding the centre forward's leg. The boot cracked into the calf of his own leg with deadening force. He gasped and threw his head up. Somewhere in the back of his mind he heard Georgie's voice.

'The man in the car, that's him! Look out boss!'

But Sam was too knocked about now to move. A boot smashed against his ribs and he felt his whole stomach roll.

He saw dimly the referee in the midst of the blue shirts. And he saw one of the men who had been on the side of the line fighting his way in. Voices were raised in uproar. And again he felt a boot fly at his arm. Under him Georgie crouched and the shouts were menacing and disgusting.

It was dark on the ground in the middle of the mob. Then there was a roar that stopped everything.

'Get out of it!'

Suddenly bodies began to be thrown aside and thundering into the group came Mr Goode.

'Bloody savages', he roared, 'get out of it.' Things suddenly went black.

Sam saw daylight again and felt someone leaning over him. It was the stranger on the line. Sam looked about him still dazed. Georgie was standing above him. So too were the rest of the Drove's End team. A cold sponge was being held to his forehead. Someone offered him a bottle of water. And slowly he came to, shaking his head. It was like a weight had been placed on his forehead. His ribs ached and his leg was pounding with pain.

'Are you all right, boss', Georgie was kneeling beside him. 'Are you all right.'

Sam put his hand over his face. 'I think so.' He looked around him. 'What happened?'

The man who was kneeling beside him spoke. 'Well you took a fair old battering there', he said. 'And then you passed out.'

'The match . . .' Sam started to ask, 'the match . . .'

'That was no match', said the man, 'it was a slaughter-house. Someone seemed to set you up for a fall.'

Realisation of the whole affair began to come back to Sam. He started to push himself up off the ground. 'Where are they, where are they?' He looked around – but there was no sign of any players in Blue. Then over by the hedge he saw some men disappear.

He started to pull up. His temper flared again. 'There they are . . . get them', but he wobbled back to the ground.

Mr Goode bent down. 'Don't worry, Mr Nelson', he said, 'it's all over. Called off . . .'

'Yes', said the stranger, 'and the referee was first to vanish.'

'It seems as though we're in the middle of a hornet's nest', said Mr Goode. 'It's another episode in the whole affair. It looks as though someone really has it in for Drove's End in general . . .'

'. . . and me in particular', interjected Georgie.

CHAPTER 7

'Watch out for Smokey Joe'

The two men helped Sam to walk to the hut. He only felt the pain in his leg and the dull ache in his ribs. It had been suggested that they should get him to a doctor but Sam wouldn't have any of it. Similarly when someone mentioned getting the police Sam wouldn't have it.

As they walked to his house from the ground Sam gave the two men his reasons for not calling in the police.

'It all began in such a small way', he said, 'there really is nothing to put your finger on. There was an offer to

Georgie – that wasn't criminal. There was the chase home . . . nothing to pin on anyone and then there was the row during the match.'

'And that row during the match could have ended much worse than it did', the stranger said. 'Your friend here', he indicated Mr Goode, 'certainly routed them. When he got amongst them they realised that there was a big gap between the men and the boys.'

'It all happened so quickly', said Sam. 'I realised as soon as I saw the big fellow wrestling with Georgie what had happened. I had to go out . . .'

'He would have been a much sorrier lad today but for you', said Mr Goode.

Sam began to feel life returning now to his limbs. He looked at the stranger.

'I thought you came with them', he said.

The man laughed. 'Well I suppose I did – but it only happened that I'm from Brimsley like most of those you played against . . .'

'Say that again . . . slowly', said Sam.

'I said that I'm from Brimsley . . . like most of those you played against today.'

Sam looked at him, wondering more and more was he hearing things. 'But they told me they were from Hunstanton.'

'The only time they see Hunstanton is in the summer when they go for a day trip', replied the man. 'Look my name is Paul Moffatt. I'm sports reporter on the *Chronicle*.'

Sam nodded.

'I came here today to look over your lads before their game with Brimsley Boys next week – and instead I find myself in the middle of a minor war.'

'You know all that's happening then.'

'Well most of it anyway . . . and maybe a little more.'

'More?' asked Mr Goode.

'Well, I saw your lad Georgie over at Brimsley's ground a couple of nights ago. He was looking for Smokey Joe.'

'And he found him', said Mr Goode with a grimace.

Sam shifted himself on the stool; he didn't think a mere kick in the ribs could make you feel so bad. And the whole affair was getting just too much for him. Surely there must be someone somewhere who could give him the simple answer what it was all about.

They told the reporter about the chase home and how they were invited to take part in the sponsored game.

The reporter stood looking at them. There was a sudden drift of something big in front of him now. Loose ends began to tie themselves up automatically for him. Smokey Joe . . . the Brimsley reserve players he had spotted in the All-Blues . . . the chase to get Georgie . . . it seemed all to centre round the boy. And because he knew Brimsley so well he knew just what the link was. There had been rumours before other games . . . Smokey Joe – and the glory loving Mr Bradshaw.

He remembered now his own conversation with Bradshaw a while earlier outside the restaurant. Georgie had been mentioned then. There was something more than a good story here – there was the link with so many mysterious results before.

Sam began to move on the bench. 'I suppose we ought to make our way home', he said, 'after all there's only another week to survive.'

But Paul Moffatt caught his arm and put him sitting down again.

'I'm sure I don't have to spell it out to you just what is happening', he said to Sam. 'But whenever there is a chance of glory from Brimsley Boys there is bad news for anyone that gets in their way.'

Mr Goode stood up and Sam recognised all the old fury he knew the man was capable of. 'You wouldn't mean that as a threat . . .'

The stranger held up his hand. 'Now Mr Goode, take it easy. I'm on your side.'

The big man stood still.

'This is intimidation on the usual scale', he told them. 'Brimsley Boys are poised for Europe. I wonder if you saw my story a while ago in which I reported that Bradshaw, the man who runs the Boys, was so sure of getting to Europe with his team that he has already made provisions for the visas?'

'I did', said Sam, gingerly touching his ribs.

'Well the same Mr Bradshaw would be the laughing stock of the whole town if he was proved wrong. I would watch myself for the rest of the week . . . and I'd watch out for Smokey Joe.'

'Smokey Joe had better watch out for me', Sam winced with the pain. 'We're old enemies. I still have marks from his over-the-top tackles on my legs. Oh yes there's little love between Smokey Joe and myself.'

'Bradshaw is still going to try and stop Georgie lining out in that game next week. He has to – because he won't be able to pull any dirty tricks on the field. This time there will be a genuine referee and the teams will be evenly matched. He will still try to make it tough for Georgie and he is never lost for stooges.'

Sam and Mr Goode looked at each other. Sam shook his head. 'Maybe it would be better for the lads if we opted out of the game. I've had enough of this . . .'

'Well we haven't . . .' the three men swung around to

the door of the hut where four of the players were standing, now fully dressed. It was Georgie who spoke. 'We heard all that was said, and no matter what happens we will be out on that pitch next week-end.'

'And we're going to win', said Derek Quick.

Sam laughed . . . but it was the laugh that did it. He let out a cry and fell to the floor. The men bent over him and the boys rushed in.

The reporter looked up. 'He's out for six', he said. 'It's a hospital job now. One of you run and phone for an ambulance.'

CHAPTER 8

'At least go down fighting'

Drove's End is a part of the world where hooliganism is a term that is applied to the big towns and cities. That it should invade their own village was a shock to everyone. Long before Monday's *Chronicle* hit the streets the villagers knew all the details of the assault on Sam and the team. They knew too that the team manager had been taken to hospital and was unlikely to be out in less than ten days. Cracked rib, bruised, battered and shocked was the non-medical message that was passed around from person to person.

For all that the *Chronicle* story of the whole affair was avidly read.

'Football team manager savaged', read the headline on the story that was given front page space:

A small Fenland village's triumphant football team fell
victim to a gang of thugs on Saturday. And no one on the
team knows the reason why. Drove's End, winners of the
Fenland schoolboy league last season met a team called
All-Blues in a match they were told was part of a league
winner's Plaque competition. The All-Blues turned out to
be a made-up team of players, all four to five years older
than Drove's End's fifteen-year-olds. The game was only
minutes old when the local centre forward, Georgie
Goode, was attacked by an All-Blues player. Mr Sam
Nelson, manager of the Droves End team, rushed to
intervene but was kicked and beaten so badly that he was
taken to the General Hospital where he has been detained
with, among other injuries, a cracked rib. People at
Drove's End were reluctant to place the blame at anyone's
door but they did suggest that there must be an element of
jealousy in the whole affair. Their boys team has been
providing some local thrills and on Saturday meet
Brimsley Boys in the final of the County Cup.
After Saturday's amazing attack it is doubtful whether
there will be a game as Drove's End wonder boy, Georgie
Goode, was also injured in the melee and may not be able
to play.

Councillor Bradshaw threw down the paper.

'Well you got that one right, anyway', he said to
Smokey Joe. 'But your lads nearly went too far.'

'Never too far where Sam Nelson is concerned', laughed
Joe. 'That was a bonus for myself.'

'From now on keep away from here', said Bradshaw.
'And no matter what happens you keep your mouth shut
about our arrangement.'

'I'll do that, I'll do that', Joe answered enthusiastically.

'Right, get off with you then', Bradshaw began to work on some papers at his desk. He looked up annoyed when Joe didn't move. 'Hop it, Joe. I don't want anyone to get ideas about our relationship.'

Joe shifted his feet. 'Well what about the money, Mr Bradshaw . . .'

'You'll get it later', said Bradshaw.

'But I have to pay the lads. A fiver each.'

Bradshaw stood up from the desk.

'Well pay them Joe, I'm not stopping you. But there won't be any money from me until the whole thing has

blown over. I want to make sure that we win that match –
and then you'll get your money.'

'How can I be sure I'll get it', Joe whined.

'You can't Joe . . . you can't. Go on . . . out.' Bradshaw
moved threateningly around to Joe. But the little man
held his place.

'I'm afraid, Mr Bradshaw, that I can't pay the lads . . .
and it's not worth my life to go back and tell them they're
not being paid. You know that one of them had to have
stitches put in his face from a blow he got from a man at
Drove's End.'

'He should be more subtle', Bradshaw said quietly.
'And so should you Joe. You wouldn't like me to let it be
known in certain quarters that you were responsible for
setting up the match; that you put the advertisement in
the *Chronicle*. That you arranged the referee. That you
arranged the players. Would you?'

'You can't prove it', Joe shouted.

'Now keep your voice down or I will have to send for
help.'

'I'll tell them about your part in it all.'

'Oh, no you won't Joe. Who would believe a snivelling
little creature like you?'

Bradshaw moved closer to Joe. 'Now be a good boy Joe
and hop it. Quick.'

Joe shuffled backwards towards the door.

'That's a good fellow, Mr Sherman', Bradshaw said
loudly. 'I'm afraid there is nothing I can do to help you.
But do come back and see me when the situation has
resolved itself. It will be a pleasure to do business with
you.'

And with that he gave Joe a gentle push out the door
and closed it loudly behind him.

Paul Moffatt sat down beside Sam's hospital bed. Sam smiled at his query as to how he felt.

'I never thought they could wrap you up so tight', he said, 'or that bruises could hurt so much.'

'Have they said how long you'll be here?' asked the newspaperman.

'Ten days at least', Sam said ruefully. 'Which means there's no County Final for me on Saturday. I wonder how they'll do.'

'They'll do all right', said Paul, 'wait until you see them coming in here on Saturday night with the cup.'

Sam began to laugh. 'Ouch', he said, 'a laugh is punishment just now.'

Paul took up a paper he had brought with him. 'Have you seen this yet?' he pointed out the story to Sam. The Irishman shook his head. 'Well you had better read it then . . . and don't get excited until we've talked about it.'

Sam read the story. As he went down through it he showed no rection until he came close to the end.

'What's this about Georgie?' he turned a worried look at Paul.

'That's why I told you not to get excited. Now you might say that was a little bit of journalistic licence . . . he did get a kick during the fight . . . but he is quite well. There's no chance of him not playing on Saturday.'

Sam nodded his understanding.

'Mr Goode agreed that I should say that in the story – it might keep things quieter for young Georgie during the week. Agree?'

'I do indeed', said Sam, 'thanks.'

'Thanks for nothing', said the newspaperman. 'After all we owe it to you. We printed the advertisement for the match – in good faith mind you – so the least we

can do is to help you with a little white lie this time.'

'I'd hate to think that anything else could happen to Georgie', said Sam. 'I wonder who has it in for us.'

'That's something I'm working on', said Paul. 'This thing is a lot bigger than you think it is. The police have been on to me . . . have they been to see you?'

'They have', Sam replied, 'but there was little I could do to help.'

'Well I know they are certainly going to take up the whole thing – and probably by the end of the week they will know something.'

'But will that be soon enough?' Sam tried to shift his body in the bed but the pain was too much.

'It will be soon enough if they can make Smokey Joe tell them the whole story. I've also given them a few names of lads who turned out for the All-Blues against you. But the one who made the attack was a stranger to me – I wouldn't say he was a footballer at all. A heavy, I wouldn't be surprised, with no other motivation than the price he was being paid for the job.'

'Smokey Joe's the link all right', agreed Sam. 'But he isn't so thick that he would be carrying over our feud of years ago and take it out on the lads . . . would he?'

'That's something only time will tell. You just settle yourself down now . . . and don't worry. Mr Goode is watching over your lads and I'm betting that no one will get within a field's length of any of them for the rest of the week. As for Georgie he won't be seen doing anything that a lad with an injured leg shouldn't be doing.'

The story in the paper had the effect of bringing out a small crowd of locals to see the Drove's End boys training that evening. There had been little local interest at all in the team up to now; to most of the inhabitants they were just another crowd of boys interested in kicking a ball about and having the occasional game on the field at the end of the village. Now there was a greater interest and they watched the boys training and brought an air of new attention to the small ground.

Georgie stood beside his father. He felt a strong impulse to get out on the field and do his share of the training. But he had been told that if he was to play his full part in the efforts of Drove's End he would have to keep away from all training for the rest of the week.

'You're fit enough anyhow', his father had said, 'and if you go training you are only leaving yourself open to another attack.'

Georgie had to agree. He realised that all the attacks made on him had been aimed at stopping him playing in the county final. It seemed so obvious now – but when it was happening he just couldn't see it. Even now however the whole point of such a determined bid to win the game at any expense seemed to be just too much.

He had discussed it with his father. But no real explanation was forthcoming. Could it be gambling on the game, they wondered. His father said no – he reasoned that men were driven more often by fear of a loss of pride, than anything else. He could only assume that this was the reason for the attacks.

'Anyway, my lad, you're not going out there to kick a ball until I'm sure there's no more chance of someone else having a go at you.'

But Georgie would have liked to have brought the team together and told them of the set-up. At least they would have trained with extra enthusiasm . . . but now all their training was half hearted. There was a complete lack of enthusiasm as they ran, did their jerks and then played about with a ball.

To the spectators it must have looked a bit pointless. Mr Goode saw what was going on too. He called the team together.

'It's nothing to do with me but the way you are training out there does you little good. Put a bit of zest into it.'

He looked around the uninterested faces. 'Come on you owe it to Mr Nelson.'

'That's all right', said Derek Quick, 'but what hope have we got if we haven't got Mr Nelson here – and we won't have Georgie either. What hope have we of winning.'

'With that attitude you don't stand much chance', said Mr Goode angrily. 'Get out there and put a bit of life into it. At least you can go down fighting.'

But the training stint still went on in a desultory way and soon the boys made their way back to the hut to change and go home. Georgie went with them. They were very quiet. None of the old banter that had come even in days of trouble. Never had they been faced with a situation like this.

They quietly changed and tidied up the hut.

Suddenly Georgie felt he had to give them back some of their spirit. He was on the point of telling them everything when his father appeared at the door. 'Come on Georgie, home. And you lads', he looked around the room, 'all of you make your way straight home. No sense in leaving ourselves open to further trouble.'

There was a knock outside the door. Mr Goode went to it . . . Mrs Nelson looked in.

'Sam sends his regards', she said. 'He's looking forward to you bringing the cup to him on Saturday night.'

The boys looked at her.

'And', she said, 'you're now all under the eyes of the law.

The police may want to ask you some questions about Saturday's game . . . and they will be making sure that no one molests you for the next few days anyway.'

There was a general outbreak of talking.

'A personal bodyguard', joked Benny May. 'Local P.C. forty-nine gets his big chance. His mind was on other things when he was chasing me out of the orchard last year!'

A wave of laughter swept the lads.

'That's the spirit lads', Mr Goode said, 'and don't forget it's just a game.'

'Where have I heard that before?' asked Roy Carew. And the laughter went around the hut.

'Tell Mr Nelson that we'll bring him a cup on Saturday', said Derek Quick, 'it may not be the County Cup but we'll bring him a cup anyway!'

CHAPTER 9

'A place in the record books'

The gaiety at the end of that first night's training without Sam Nelson soon dissipated. It was decided that they would get together every night for a restricted training session. There was the feeling that everyone wanted to know how Georgie was getting on – whether there was any sign at all of his injury improving. But Georgie was there all the time, on the sideline, standing by his father's side.

Mr Goode did little and said less. He was completely out of his element and there was nothing he could do to help them with their training; there was nothing he could say that would make them work with greater enthusiasm. And no one knew it better than himself.

'You had better look on me as a watch dog', he tried to joke. 'But when it comes to training and tactics it's entirely up to you.'

The greatest hope came to them on the Thursday evening. Derek Quick had been selected as the one to go and visit Sam in hospital. A whip round had got together enough to buy a large bottle of minerals, a copy of *The Glory Game* by Hunter Davis, and four packets of polo mints – Sam's favourite sweets.

Derek had gone to the hospital on Wednesday evening and reported back to the team that Sam was well on the road to recovery.

'But he still looks shook', said Derek. 'There's enough bandage around his ribs to mark out a pitch.'

Sam sent them words of encouragement. He told them that they had played most matches so far without any real knowledge of the team they had to face; that there was no such thing as a plan as far as he was concerned.

'He says that he wants us out there to defend when we have to but to attack all the time', reported Derek.

'But what does he say about Georgie?'

'He didn't seem as worried about that as we are', Derek looked slightly puzzled. 'He said that even with ten men we could win the match.'

'He must be joking', snapped Brian Monroe.

There seemed to be general agreement about this comment. But on the outskirts of the discussion Mr Goode was hovering.

'Confidence is worth a goal start', he said, surprising himself that he should be making any comment.

Confidence however was at a low ebb that night. It was being eaten away by all the other happenings of the previous days. Statements had been made to the police; parents had been in a very questioning mood and there was a tenseness about everything from school work to bedtime. Even the fact that now more and more parents and friends were visiting the ground every evening ... and as far as the boys were concerned were seeing little progress in the team's workouts.

The villagers gathered in small knots around the ground and were frequently joined by P.C. Thomson, the local policeman, who spent a lot of his spare time keeping a watchful eye on the proceedings. To the boys it seemed a lot of work – for little return.

For all that there were some very definite moves that set up conversation among the boys. A mini bus was hired to take them to the match on Saturday. A whole contingent of parents and friends were going ... and even the ten year olds in the village school were organising a party.

'Why didn't they do it for a match we were likely to win', muttered Benny May, 'like when we won the League'.

Gloom was almost an overaweing presence among the team especially as the *Chronicle* continued to print snippets of information about the game and the incidents of the previous week.

'Brimsley Boys at full strength for big game.'

'Drove's End star still misses training.'

'Police want to interview man about match attack.'

The headlines went through the week. Admittedly they were small items in the main sports news ... but they were read more avidly for all that. And only a few people knew that there was more to read into them than the headlines seemed to say.

Sam in his hospital bed remained as confident as he could. He was helped by pain killing drugs and sleeping tablets that kept the cold thoughts of night away from him. He was helped too by the messages his wife brought him from the boys and by the visit of Derek Quick. Then there wasn't a day when Paul Moffatt didn't come in to talk to him and keep him right up to date with the latest developments in the police issue.

The police came too . . . but they didn't give him any

information, just questions. Questions that became deeper and more probing as the week wore on.

By Thursday they had brought in full details of Sam's own footballing career and had found newspaper reports of a game where the rivalry of Sam and Joe Sherman was the main talking point. How Sam had led the other man a dance all through the game, only to be sliced down by a tackle that not only marked his leg but finished with a kick in the mouth that lost two precious teeth. And then there was the subsequent newspaper cutting that showed that Joe had been banned for six months for the assault.

Indeed it seemed as though there was little the police did not know. Only one question puzzled Sam. 'Do you know Councillor Bradshaw?' And Sam answered in the negative. The question was repeated and followed up by another – 'would Councillor Bradshaw have any reason for disliking you or young Goode?'

At first Sam answered no – then he added that the only reason was likely to be the match on Saturday. Maybe Councillor Bradshaw wanted Brimsley Boys to win it – at any price.

The policeman showed no particular interest to Sam's reply. Just nodded and made another note in the book.

And Sam was left wondering. He really missed the team, the training nights, the exciting build-up to the final. That was the involvement he liked. All the time there was something new to try out; some little move that came back to him through the haze of his past footballing career, something that he would have liked to try out; to attempt with the boys. But all he was left with was the nothingness of a soft green ward wall and frightening vision of all that had happened only a few days ago. A few days . . . they seemed like eternity.

Even the thought of having to wait until Saturday evening for the final result of the game upset him, it seemed so far away; so helplessly out of his reach. And all the time the dull thudding in his ribs and muscles reminded him of it; every time he moved he saw that big centre half descend again on Georgie. There was only one consolation – he had seen it in time.

Friday evening Sam was sitting up in his bed, as tense as ever and only one thought in his mind . . . what was happening at Drove's End. The attacks and even his own injuries had slipped into the back of his mind and he didn't give himself any time to think of them. Tonight he should be there, encouraging, suggesting and making sure that everything was in order for the next day. After all it was the biggest day in the whole story of Drove's End. The League win had been exhilarating – but the County Cup, now that was something altogether different. Even the fact that the team was in the final was enough to celebrate . . . but in there with a chance to win . . .

He shook his head. Win? Well in the silence of a hospital bed he could afford to be pessimistic . . . it would be a different tale if he was there at Drove's End. He had heard so much about these Brimsley Boys since he came to hospital that he didn't want to hear another mention of the name.

In the town there was a genuine enthusiasm for the local boys. They were without doubt the headline snatchers of all the local schoolboy teams and had left a trail of well beaten teams behind them on their record unbeaten run. He reckoned that the *Guinness Book of Records* should have heard of them. He had a nurse bring him a copy and looked up the best winning run for a boy's team.

There it was a Yorkshire team, Laughton Boys, with thirty-seven wins in thirty-seven matches . . . surely Brimsley Boys must be close to this now. He checked his facts – thirty-six games without losing! Now Saturday's game would have then equalling the record. Maybe that

73

was what spurred on Councillor Bradshaw. A place in Europe and a place in the *Guinness Book of Records*!

Out of curiosity he read the rest of the entry – it was about a team that he had heard of – Nomads F.C. who played in the Norwich Lads League and had gone twenty matches without a win! But it was the rest of the entry that caught his attention. It said that their goals tally was eleven for, 431 against 'despite buying a new goalkeeper for twenty-five pence!'

He laughed and noticed that the twinge in his side was nowhere near as bad as it had been. If only Georgie knew that fifty pence was double the going rate for a prospective match winner!

He was still smiling to himself when Paul Moffatt came up to his bed.

'Well Sam that's a nice change, to see you smiling.'

Sam laughed again and told Paul the reason for his smiles.

'And I'll give you something else to make you smile', Paul settled himself on the side of the bed. 'The police have charged the man who hit you. He was from Middlestone over in Northamptonshire and a well known heavy. And they've charged Smokey Joe with being an accessory.'

Sam looked wide-eyed. 'That will stop them getting at the team now', he said.

'I think so', said Paul, 'and it may also sober up Councillor Bradshaw for I've a feeling that Smokey Joe will talk like a parrot as soon as the pressure is on.'

He stood up to leave. 'I have to hurry . . . and good luck tomorrow. You never know what might happen now.'

CHAPTER 10

'*A song to remember*'

The songs they sang in the bus on the way to Brimsley were home made versions of the countless songs that they associated with football grounds and teams light years away from Drove's End. Adapted they sang 'Nice one Georgie'. 'When the Drovers go marching in' and many more. Only when they reached 'We are the Champions' did someone suggest that it wasn't right to count their goals before they were scored.

The songs helped to keep the tension down in the bus. It was a tension that hadn't been helped by the absence of Sam; by the lack of communication from Mr Goode; by the fact that they weren't sure what the team was going to be; by the presence of the perpetual sub, Hugh Richards, who took his place on the sideline now as much a part of the team as one of the boys on the field. No one mentioned to Hugh that this was to be his day. And had they said anything they would only have received a nod from the substitute. He knew more than anyone else there outside Mr Goode and Georgie.

By the time they had reached Brimsley they had run out of songs. They were very quiet and very tense as the bus pulled up outside the Town's ground. A small knot of boys stood around the entrance and set up a shout as the Drove's End boys arrived. There was a half hearted attempt at a jeer as the players got off the bus . . . and passed by into the office and through a corridor to a dressing room. As they walked into the dressing room

Georgie suddenly realised that this was where he had seen Smokey Joe. He thought he could still get the whiff of his foul smelling tobacco.

Mr Goode carried the bag that Sam Nelson had used to bring the gear in for a long time now. The big man looked ill at ease and felt it too. He was lost for words and still felt the anger bottled up inside him . . . anger at whoever it was that went so much out of their way to try and upset the Drove's End dreams and hopes.

He put the bag down and the boys sat on benches, looking at each other in a slightly embarrassed way. Mr Goode hovered about, wondering what to do and when to do it. He looked at his watch. Half an hour to kick-off time. It was too long to wait. But he was determined that no one would go outside the dressing room until it was time to go out for the game.

'Shall we start to get stripped?' asked Derek Quick.

Mr Goode hesitated. 'Isn't it too soon?' he asked.

'Not the way some of these put on their gear', replied Roy Carew.

'O.K. then, start getting dressed then', Mr Goode moved about and tried to fidget in the big bag.

Then came the question that he had hoped would be put off for a while.

'What's the team?' asked Benny May.

Everyone was very quiet – looking at the big man. Mr Goode took a piece of paper from his pocket.

'Mr Nelson picked the team', he said, 'it's the same team that played in the last game.'

The players looked bewildered.

'That isn't possible', said Derek, 'what about Georgie? Who is playing in his place.'

Father and son looked at each other. Then with a wild

whoop Georgie jumped up. 'I'm in', he shouted and did a double jump. Then as everyone looked at him he sat down.

He looked around the rest of his team mates.

'I wasn't really hurt', he explained. 'It was just a way to keep me out of trouble.'

There was a general outburst of pleasure. Everyone seemed to be talking at once . . . and laughing . . . and it was a very different crowd of boys now who faced up to the game.

'But, I want you all to listen to me', said Mr Goode. 'Our troubles may not be over yet. No one leaves this dressing room without me . . . and only then for the very best of reasons. We all go out there on the pitch together. And until we're out there I don't expect anyone to know that Georgie will be playing.'

There were nods of acceptance and Jimmy Neil added: 'They'll know it soon enough, Mr Goode!' and he shook his head in a personal sort of disbelief.

The strip was handed out; the old bantering returned and Mr Goode stationed himself by the door. But the only knock was from the referee who came in and asked if everything was all right. He looked about him searchingly . . . as if expecting to see trouble somewhere in the room.

'I've heard a lot about you lads', he said. 'You certainly got your share of the publicity before the match. Go out there and forget it ever happened. Play this match as you would any other . . . play fair with me and I'll promise you that everyone will play fair with you.'

He turned and walked out the door with a final 'good luck'.

It was the referee who called them to go out on the pitch. Down the long tunnel and out into the bright sunlight. On to a ground where a few hundred spectators had gathered. And a great shout went up from a section of the stands where most of the people of Drove's End had stationed themselves.

The boys kicked a ball in front of them and ran towards the goal. They didn't see the agitated group standing on the stand steps.

Mr Edward Bradshaw was one of them . . . and unmistakeably there too was Smokey Joe. And there were two other men. Voices were being raised. Mr Bradshaw's face was a deep red . . . he was wildly shaking a fist at Smokey Joe. He pointed to the field . . . and one of the men caught Smokey Joe's arm and led him out. Councillor Bradshaw half stumbled to a seat in the stand . . . face red with fury.

Brimsley Boys ran on to the field to the accompaniment of a blare of bugles on the amplifier system. And a shout went up from the locals. The boys of Drove's End turned to see their opponents for the first time.

'They look the right size this time anyway', laughed John Macken from the goalmouth.

'But where have I seen that strip before?' Derek Quick brought the players to a standstill. The All-Blue outfit looked suspiciously familiar. 'The Blue Canaries', someone laughed.

'Maybe it's just another move to try and frighten us', said Benny May.

Georgie stood looking, a frown on his face. A frown that was taking on that almost wild look that the boys at Drove's End had come to accept was a part of the centre forward when he was annoyed. They saw it too in Georgie's father. And they saw too the same reluctance to talk under pressure . . . very much like father like son.

'Forget them', urged Roy Carew, 'let's remember that this is a game we're going to win.'

He raced at the ball and tucked it neatly into the farthest corner of the net to the accompaniment of a boo from the crowd behind the goal.

But there was nothing said, no sign by any of the team in the all white that they had heard anything.

Derek Quick lost the toss and the Brimsley Boys' captain

decided to play the way the teams were. He looked at Derek Quick. 'It won't make much difference to us', he said, 'we'll score in any of them.'

The referee pulled him up. 'Less of that', he said, and added 'I don't want any dirty play here.'

'We're not dirty', sneered the Brimsley captain. 'Just frightening.'

He backed off as the referee shook an admonishing finger at him. Derek Quick stood his ground, and smiled in a tantalising way at the opposing captain.

'We'll wipe that smile off your face', came the retort.

As if to carry out the full force of their own words Brimsley went into the tackle straight away, taking the ball away from the astonished Chris May with almost brute strength. The force of the tackle swung the Drove's End lad to the ground and the ball pitched right forward. Brimsley Boys ran it, a full sweep of forwards bearing down in formation against the Drove's End defence.

Derek Quick himself stood bewildered as the ball was neatly taken around him. Only John Macken was left.

The goalkeeper ran from his line just as the Brimsley forward shot, hard and knee high at the open goal. A frantic dive by the goalkeeper found the ball . . . but it was only a one handed effort, the ball ran loose and the forward following up, ran it arrogantly into the net.

He kicked it twice again into the net as his supporters roared. Then he picked up the ball, ran up to the goalkeeper and brandished it under his nose.

'Better touch it now, it's the only chance you'll get other than picking it out of the net.'

The Brimsley boy laughed and threw the ball then up field.

He was surrounded by his own players as the fans

chanted 'easy, easy, easy'. And in the back rows of the stand the supporters of Drove's End were just as stunned as their team. Ten seconds gone and a goal down. It was inconceivable.

Georgie took the ball, placed it on the centre spot and restarted the game. It was almost a replica of the first move. As soon as the ball had been touched off Brimsley Boys were diving in, full of strength and ambition, intent on getting the ball. They got it and began to swing it about the field, pulling the otherwise tightly bunched Drove's End team with them, and making the boys from the Fens really put in the leg work.

Tony Merton with a long sliding tackle took the full force of the next vicious looking attack and just got the ball away from the defence. John Macken swiftly swooped on a long dropping ball that had the look of a fifty-fifty ball all the way. He grabbed the ball and just managed to side step the whirlwind advance of the centre forward who was carried past him by the momentum of the run.

But the ball stayed in the Drove's End half of the field. Two left footed shots were pumped at the vigilant Macken who held one and watched the other run past a post far too close for comfort. The centre half and the captain came racing up with the next attack and put massive power into a shot that screeched over the bar.

Then the goalkeeper was beaten by a curling centre that just went past the post.

All the time the Fenland boys fought for the ball, but there was a dreadful pall hanging over them. It seemed that no matter what they did the ball was destined to stay in their own half. And the force of the attacking Brimsley was always vigorous but somehow managed to stay on the right side of the referee who kept well up with the play.

But there seemed little cohesion in the Fenland play. They weren't being allowed to put it together and the game became a blue tide towards the Drove's End goal. Somehow though the ball stayed out of the net more than once.

Brian Munroe ran back and worked hard. Georgie too came back into his own half . . . but Georgie had never been any good in the defence. He ran and ran and chased and harried but never got an opportunity to advance with the ball for the first ten minutes.

It was a sudden shout from the sideline that came in a moment of quiet that caused the stir.

'You're playing like my granny – and she's dead this ten years!'

Only one man had ever shouted that at Drove's End boys before. Only one man would still have the lungs to raise his voice and carry it right around and across the

ground . . . so that to some of the players it seemed as though there might well have been an echo at work.

Sam Nelson. Everyone realised it at the same time. Then they realised where he was. In an invalid chair on the sideline! Waving a fist in agitation and berating them in terms that they had heard before – often and often.

'Tackle hard.' The advice came. 'Loosen up that defence.' 'Spread the ball.' 'Mind your back!' Encouraging, helping but at the same time suggesting they were blind – and slow.

But the conceited look was still there, evident in every move that Brimsley made on the ball.

Derek Quick made a wild kick at the ball and it spun out near Sam. 'You should be in the wheelchair', Sam roared at the captain.

Derek threw up his hands to his head. And just then the ball landed at his feet again. This time he stopped it, dragged it to one side to avoid the scything tackle and pumped it forward.

'Go Georgie, go!' came the cry from the wheelchair.

And Georgie went. He swept the ball ahead of him, then turned it neatly to Brian Munroe. Just the two of them running against the defence that had spent most of its time ball-watching up to this.

Brian collected his piercing pass and held it – just long enough before knocking a perfect pass to Georgie. The centre forward, long hair streaming behind him, ran like a gazelle and met the ball perfectly. It soared up and away, beyond the keeper's reach to crack off the upright.

Drove's End became all energy, dangerous crosses floated over from the touchline, runs were made down the middle, dashes were made back to help out in defence. Whereas there had only been a defence and an out of work forward line a few minutes before there now was a footballing team. And Georgie was in his element – a cunning back heel, a darting run that often left defenders helpless, and all the time the urgent need to have the ball.

But Brimsley were equal to it all. The one goal they had scored so easily was still worth the cup to them. Something like that wasn't going to be thrown away so easily. At half time they were still very much the favourites to hold out.

What must have surprised the Brimsley supporters was the action of the Drove's End boys at half time, immediately the whistle sounded they ran, full out to the sideline where they gathered round Sam's wheelchair. Pushing the chair was a man whose face they knew – now they realised it was Paul Moffatt, the *Chronicle* sports reporter.

'I'll die of shame instead of broken ribs', Sam told them. 'You can do better than this. Come on, with this game before they realise that I'm not just out for a walk in the hospital grounds. If the ambulance comes here I'll be locked away for weeks.'

He laughed, felt no pain in his side – only a pain for the boys who had to struggle on the field. He knew well what it was like. He carved them up individually, however, in his old way, sparing no one as he rocked them into realisation that they could win the game.

But it was fifteen minutes of great end-to-end football before the first real scoring chance came. And it arrived at the feet of the Brimsley Boys' centre forward. He raced forward, beat the defence but there again was John Macken advancing off his line. He dived at the feet of the big Brimsley Boy, took the ball just as the boot grazed across his face. For a second he was stunned, he rose giddily, saw a white shirt on the wing and threw the ball to the feet of Chris May. The half back's appetite had been sharpened by Sam's words. And now he heard the advice roaring from the touchline. He put in a sprint, was tackled but held the ball, ran again, was tackled again, held the ball and ran again. This time the centre half was drawn towards him. From the corner of his eye he saw Georgie run. He punted the ball forward just as he was crashed to the ground by the advancing player.

Georgie saw only the ball, the advancing goalkeeper and the net. Suddenly he was filled with belief in his ability to score. He raced in to the kill – and with verve drove the ball wide of the keeper into the gaping net.

The roar that erupted was something the boys from the Fens had never heard before. The stand seemed to rattle with hundreds of banging feet, applauding hands and roaring voices.

They were level. But this was the last time Georgie was going to get free. That became evident immediately as he was pounded into the ground by two charging defenders. He picked himself out of what seemed a rugby maul, felt the moisture on his face first and then realised that his face was cut just by the eye.

The whistle had gone. The referee was looking at his face. But Georgie shook him off.

'Nothing', he said tersely, pulling himself away from the official. He wiped his face with the sleeve of his white jersey and a long streak of blood left its mark.

He was still full of running. So too were Jimmy Evans, Jimmy Neil and Brian Munroe. Derek Quick raced to the ball, played it wide to Pat Lucas and the full back's boot met it in mid-air. The ball swung high into the goalmouth. A rush of players and it was loose at Georgie's feet. All of a sudden he seemed mesmerised. He took the ball back, then forward, past one defender, almost looked for another defender. When the full back came he slyly touched the ball to one side and stepping back let the Brimsley lad thrash forward.

There was nothing mesmerised about him now. He hit the ball with a swerving shot and the goalkeeper didn't even know it was past him until he was picking it from the net.

Georgie stood his ground, amid the wild cries of delight from his team, then he ran to the sideline and shouted about the tumult.

'That was for you, boss!'

Brimsley couldn't cope with the renewed vitality of Drove's End. It became almost one way traffic . . . with the local boys packing the defence and hopefully pumping balls up the field. But there they were collected competently by the Fenland defenders . . . and driven back into the fray.

And in the middle of the battle there was Georgie, blood congealing on his face and shirt, never giving the defenders a chance.

Minutes to go and a final flurry. Again perseverance by Chris May saw him through three tackles before he turned the ball to Brian Munroe, who quickly switched it out to Benny May.

His cross was perfect, swinging away from the goal-keeper – and there was Georgie Goode, a mass of tangled black hair, leaping high to head the ball hard into the net.

The excitement was so great among the supporters in the stands that they didn't notice the arrival of a policeman accompanied by a man in a raincoat. They stepped into the front of the stand just as Councillor Bradshaw was storming out of his seat intent on leaving. Three goals to one – the humiliation was too great for him. But the meeting with the two policemen was the final disaster. They took him by the arm and led him away.

Down the pitch the final whistle went. The roaring was tumultous, congratulations were thumped on every back.

The Brimsley players moved disconsolately into their own huddle as the trophy was presented to Derek Quick. The captain held it high and then ran to the wheelchair where Sam was still sitting. He pushed the trophy at the manager. The players gathered around and then a group of singing supporters came running over.

Somewhere in the background there were voices raised in song. 'WE are the champions – Drove's End', they chanted.

And from the wheelchair the cup was thrust skywards by Sam Nelson. Then he thrust it into Georgie's hands. He looked at the boy's blood-caked face.

'How's the cut, Georgie?' he asked.

'It's nothing', said Georgie, 'nothing that a winner's medal won't cure.'